John Burningham

Mr Gumpy's Outing

RED FOX

Some other books by John Burningham

Aldo

Avocado Baby

Borka

Cloudland

Come Away From the Water, Shirley

Courtney

Edwardo

Granpa

Harquin

Humbert

Husherbye

John Patrick Norman McHennessy

The Magic Bed

Mr Gumpy's Motor Car

Oi! Get Off Our Train

Picnic

The Shopping Basket

Simp

Time to Get Out of the Bath, Shirley

Trubloff

Tug of War

Whadayamean

Where's Julius?

Would You Rather . . .

MR GUMPY'S OUTING
A RED FOX BOOK 978 0 099 40879 6

First published in Great Britain by Jonathan Cape,
an imprint of Random House Children's Publishers UK
A Random House Group Company

Jonathan Cape edition published 1970
Red Fox edition first published 2001
This edition published 2013

10 9 8 7 6 5 4 3

Red Fox Books are published by Random House Children's Publishers UK,
61–63 Uxbridge Road, London W5 5SA

www.**randomhousechildrens**.co.uk
www.**randomhouse**.co.uk

Addresses for companies within The Random House Group Limited can be found at:
www.randomhouse.co.uk/offices.htm

THE RANDOM HOUSE GROUP Limited Reg. No. 954009

A CIP catalogue record for this book is available from the British Library.

Printed in China

This is Mr Gumpy.

Mr Gumpy owned a boat and his house
was by a river.

One day Mr Gumpy went out in his boat.

"May we come with you?" said the children.

"Yes," said Mr Gumpy,
"if you don't squabble."

"Can I come along, Mr Gumpy?"
said the rabbit.

"Yes, but don't hop about."

"I'd like a ride," said the cat.

"Very well," said Mr Gumpy.
"But you're not to chase the rabbit."

"Will you take me with you?" said the dog.

"Yes," said Mr Gumpy.
"But don't tease the cat."

"May I come, please, Mr Gumpy?"
said the pig.

"Very well, but don't muck about."

"Have you a place for me?" said the sheep.

"Yes, but don't keep bleating."

"Can we come too?" said the chickens.

"Yes, but don't flap," said Mr Gumpy.

"Can you make room for me?" said the calf.

"Yes, if you don't trample about."

"May I join you, Mr Gumpy?" said the goat.

"Very well, but don't kick."

For a little while they all went along happily but then...

The goat kicked

The calf trampled

The chickens flapped

The sheep bleated

The pig mucked about

The dog teased the cat

The cat chased the rabbit

The rabbit hopped

The children squabbled

The boat tipped...

and into the water they fell.

Then Mr Gumpy and the goat and the calf and the chickens and the sheep and the pig and the dog and the cat and the rabbit and the children all swam to the bank and climbed out to dry in the hot sun.

"We'll walk home across the fields," said Mr Gumpy. "It's time for tea."

"Goodbye," said Mr Gumpy.
"Come for a ride another day."